D0680389

IF YOU FIND A UNICORN IT IS NOT YOURS TO KEEP

Life Lessons
for My Magical
Daughter

DJ CORCHIN

sourcebooks
eXplore

To Grae

My Dearest Daughter,

You were born with special, magical abilities. Although this is not unique in the world, it is not true for everyone. There is no map for the journey you will take and I cannot tell you how it will end. But I can share with you the lessons I have learned to help guide in the choices you will make. Some choices will be very difficult and you will not always get them right. Your choices, however, not your abilities will be what define you. I know I cannot prevent all the mistakes you will make, but I can help to ensure you make new ones. My mistakes are my gift to you, my amazing, magical daughter.

I love you.

When you encounter a
troll, give it a cupcake.

Every troll has a sweet side.
You might get to see it.

If you travel east beyond
the Outland Hills, you will
find a different garden.
An upside-down garden.
Some will think poorly of
it because it is different.

Good people find beauty in it.

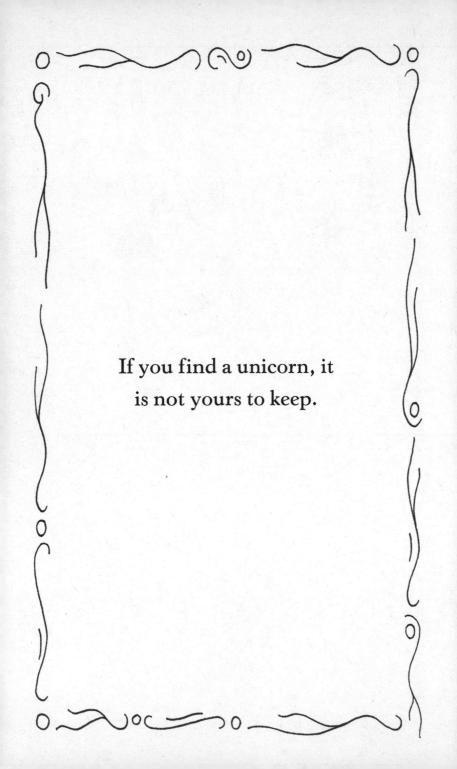

If you find a unicorn, it
is not yours to keep.

The wisest, most powerful sorcerer in the world is often found sitting in the corner of a classroom… listening, nothing more.

The Shadow Wolf lives
in the Forgotten Fields.
It is expected that if you
venture there it will eat you.
Because of this, no one has
gone there to find that the
wolf is loving and kind.

A Listening Shell of the
Narlock Folk allows you
to understand those who
speak differently than you.

Obtain one of these.

You were born with magical abilities. Some say those born with magical abilities cannot be a knight, as they are destined only to be magicfolk.

They are wrong.

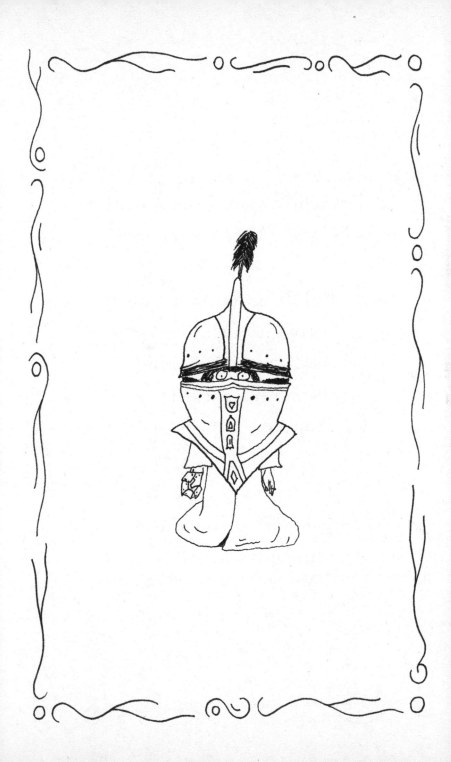

Befriend a Gnarlfish. No one speaks to it because it is a fish.

But the Gnarlfish is no ordinary fish. It sees and hears everything from underneath the surface of the lake.

It will provide you with wisdom that you will not find anywhere else.

You have a choice to cast
good spells or bad spells.

Choose good spells.

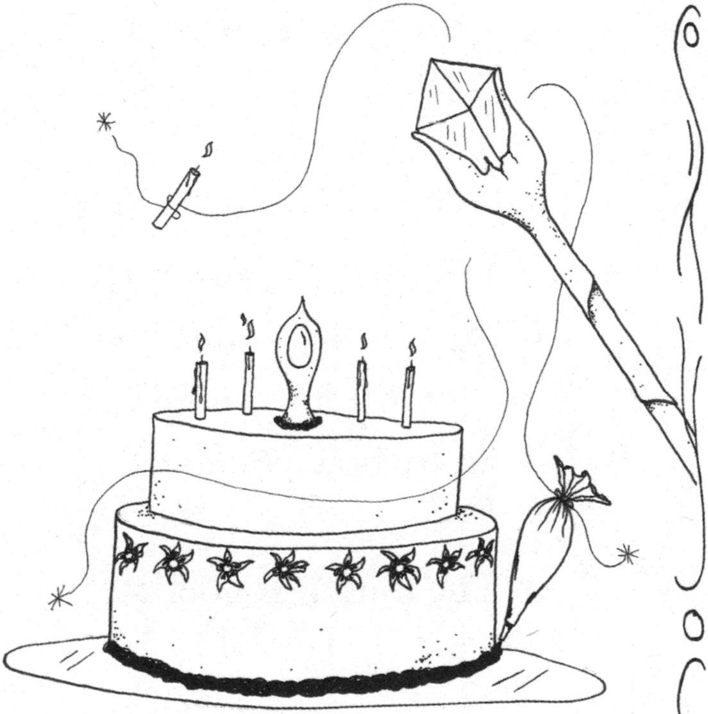

There is a mirror in the West Tower. It is the Judging Mirror. It will judge you not by whom you love, but by how you love.

The mirror is good.

The Rodent Spell, which
turns someone into a rat,
will also do the same to
the person who casts it.

Invisibility spells only
work on people who want
to learn, not on those
who want to hide.

Magic can tell.

Your dragon is a source
of great power.

Treat her well, take care
of her, and she will do
the same for you.

Legend says anyone who is
able to sit upon the Sapphire
Throne will rule the world.

If you are not worthy,
it will eat you.

Beware. It is a trick.

It eats everyone.

Sit upon the sapphire throne,
Rule the world as no one's known,
Try your luck and bet your bones,
Sit upon the sapphire throne.

The most beautiful of all
flowers only grows when the
season is too cold to bear.
You cannot stumble upon
it. It must be sought after.

It is truly wonderful to
see. I know you are worthy
enough to find it.

There is a vial hidden in
the world containing a
magical potion that gives you
everything you could ever ask
for. You can find where it is
very easily. You must journey
seventy years to get there.

Magic comes in many forms.

Not all of them require spells.

The Crimson Gem is a rare
artifact that causes others
to fall in love with the
person who possesses it.

I hope you learn enough
about the heart not to be
so naive as to seek it out.

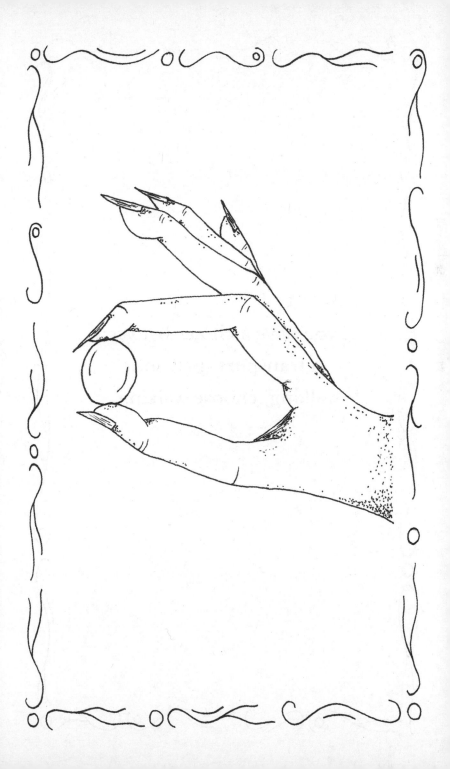

If you have a choice between
a transport spell and
walking, choose walking.

The smallest creatures in the land are the Bubble Elves that live amongst the dew. Transform yourself into one of them and live as they do. Only then will you really know about the Bubble Elves...and they will know about you.

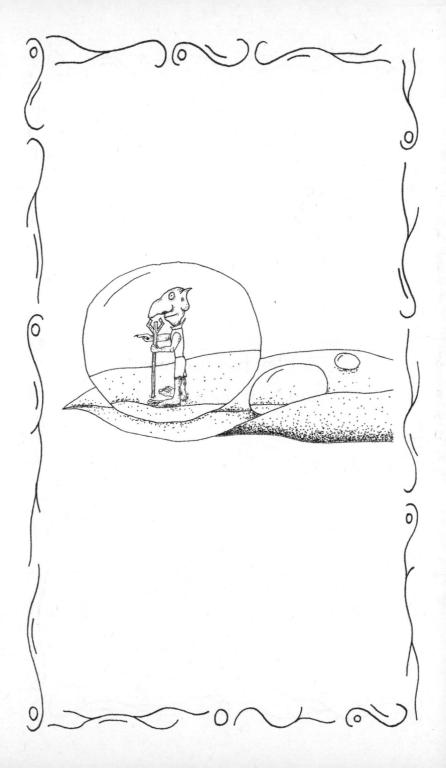

A Flen has two faces
and is never a friend.

If you find yourself in a dark
forest where the ground
engulfs you and you become
stuck, grow and be for others
the light you never had.

You will be tempted by
a Fyrkel Imp to use your
magic for personal gain when
you are alone and no one
is watching. If you refuse,
you will be rewarded in the
most beautiful of ways.

The root of the Pikerd Flower
that grows in our gardens
possesses a power that can
destroy all your enemies.
When you eat it, it enables
you to forgive those who
have wronged you when
you feel you cannot.

There is a magical instrument called the Aulos Amicus. When you play it, you will be able to see your dreams appear in images floating above you.

When you play it with others, you will see those dreams come true.

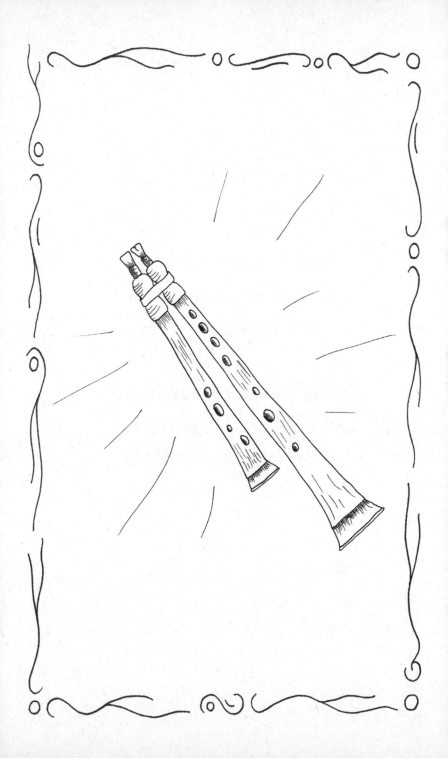

The Benzicle Beast is a
gentle, simple creature
with only one power.

If you promise it something
and do not act upon your
spoken words, it will take
away your magic.

Magical ideas come in
the form of stars.

A powerful wizard looks up
and plucks them from the sky.

A compassionate wizard
shares them with others.

A courageous wizard kneels
down so others may stand
upon her shoulders to reach.

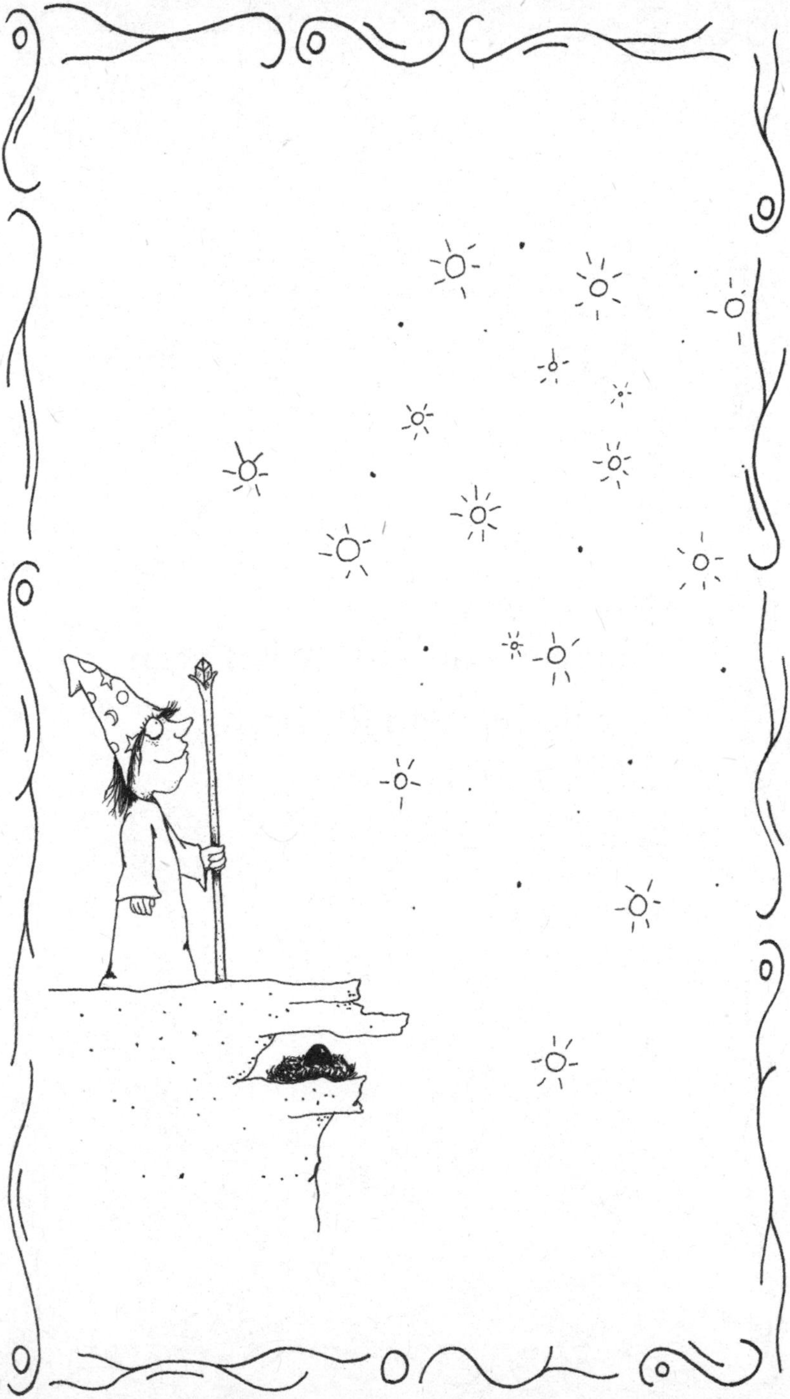

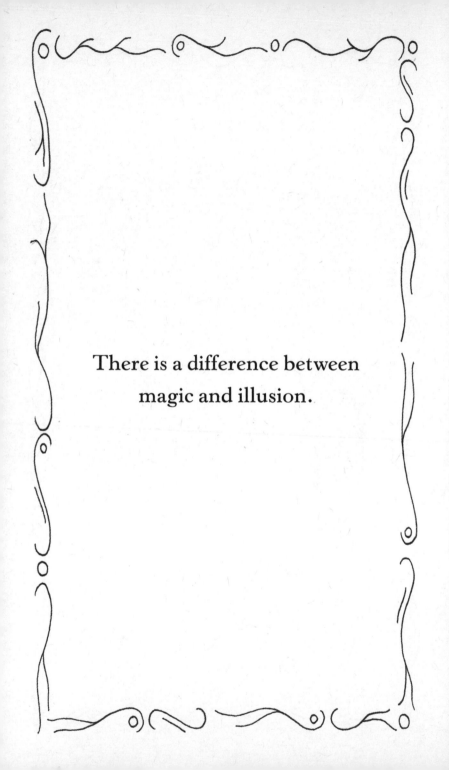

There is a difference between
magic and illusion.

There is a book called the
Magia Lux. It contains all
the magic spells in the world.
I believe you can add to it.

You should believe too.

You may come to find
a Fortune Falcon has
befriended you, giving
you the ability to see the
future. Although it may be a
welcomed guest, know that
this bird is still a wild beast.
If you mistreat it, it can claw
out your eyes and make
you blind to the present.

To enter the Labyrinth, you must appease the Mouthy Meacher who guards the entrance and never shares what it wants. It is impossible to converse with it as the Meacher never stops talking about its countless journeys. There is a tree stump just to the left. Sit there and listen attentively. That is all the Meacher needs and the door will open.

A Wishing Orb grants a wish
to the person who possesses
it. It only does so, however,
when you give the Orb away.

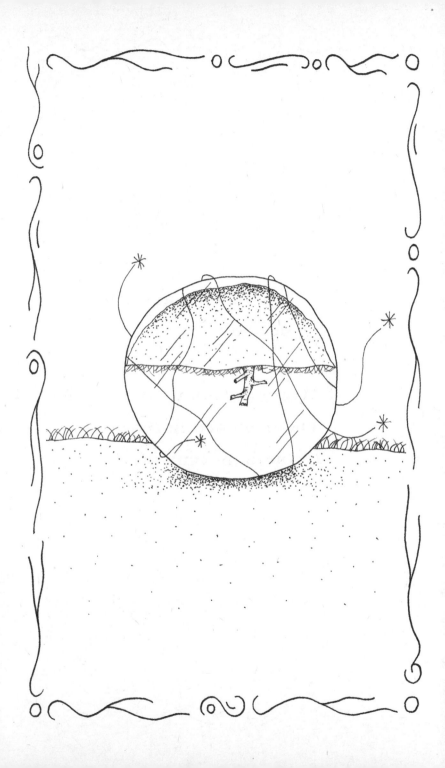

There is a magic that keeps
your body healthy.

Words are not used.
The spell is conjured
through movement.

Behind the southwest wall
in your room, you will find
a scroll. Written on it is the
Impossible Task given to me
by my grandfather whose
mother gave it to him. The
only way to accomplish it
is to never quit trying.

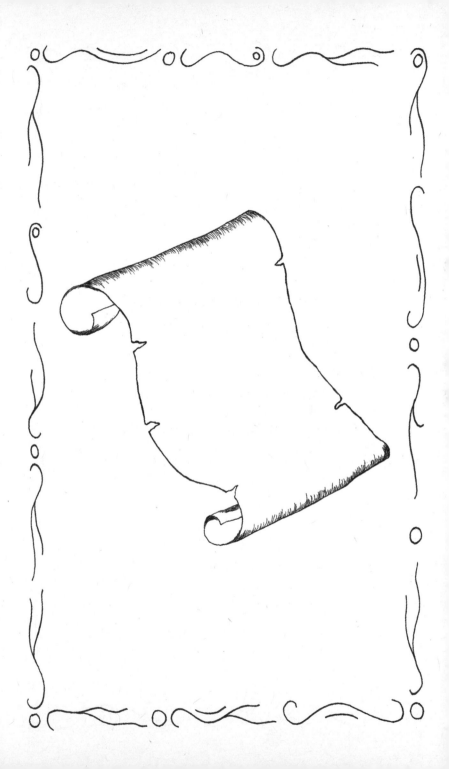

Do not fall victim to
a Flattery Spell.

But forgive those who
attempt to use it on you.

Spend a day's travel walking with the Hollyn Grae. It never stops wandering, spending its time looking for people to smile at.

It is never lonely.

No person can tell you when you are truly a wizard. You are a wizard the moment you perform your first spell.

The oldest creatures, the Ollis, have existed since the dawn of time. They only speak if they have a question.

They are happy.

Time travel is simple.

Like the Kreks of Collinston,
write a magical book and pass
it down to your children.

In the Mid Plains, there is
a tree with three heads.

One is spiteful, one is
humble, and one is bold.

They all come from
the same roots.

The Onyx and Opal Gems
are kept in a box sealed by
magic on the northernmost
isle of Dragon Peak. They
are the source of all magic.

The Onyx Gem draws its
power from those who feel
fear of what will happen.

The Opal Gem's magic
comes from those who feel
a sense of wonderment
of what could happen.

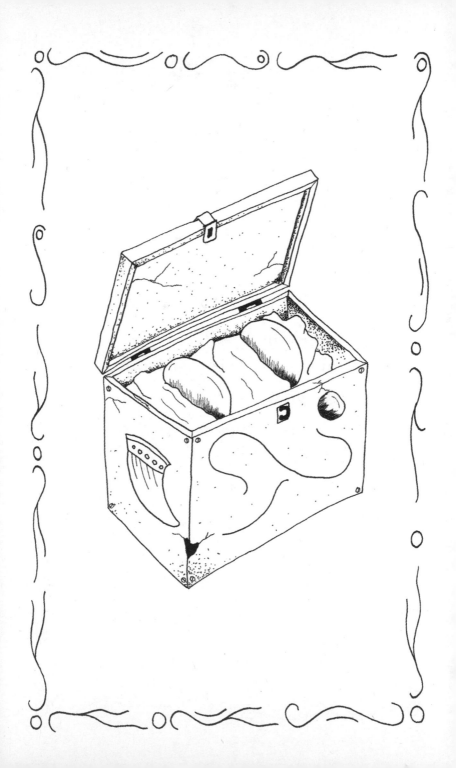

The Kolton Phoenix is not
considered magical because
of its ability to rise from
its own ashes, but because
of its choice to do so.

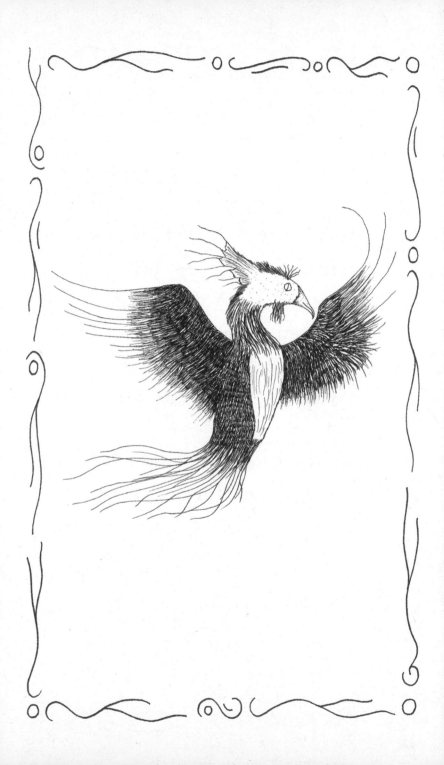

There is a wondrous butterfly
that flies into your belly
before you are about to do
something great. It may
seem like it is there to warn
you to stop, but it is not.

It is there to let you know it is
the right time for greatness.

There will be other magical folk who always disagree with your mystical ways. Love them but keep them at a distance, along with those who always agree with you.

Gimbles are the hardest
workers in the Prairie Lands.

They always take time
for a treat. They make
the best friends.

People do not know their
love of magic; they love
what they know of magic.

Show them more.

The Ancient Dark Fires of the Southern Realm burn black and cold. Any fire that burns black is not worth the pursuit.

In the Eastern Hills, there is an ancient and immortal wind that does not die and will not stop blowing. If you stand in its gusts, it will change and transform you into something better.

The more unique a creature
is the better the tale they tell.

The northeast window in the Great Library was put there by the Ancients. It is said that if a worthy person looks through it, they will see what they must do to gain happiness. The only worthy people are the ones that see their reflection in the glass.

Wands are not needed to
settle your differences.

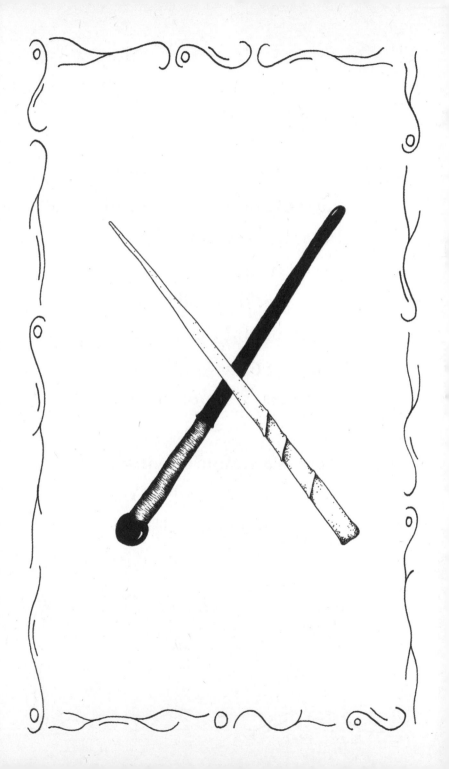

The table in the East Dining Hall is believed to have been carved from the Great Tree of Peace. It is said to have magical abilities to bring people together in the worst of times. It is not magic.

There is a simple carving on each side that reads, "You are at the same table."

The Spider Giant will help you weave an intricate, deceptive web. The spider will entrance and entice you with every strand of its beautiful silk, making you unaware of what is really happening. It is preparing to devour you. Better to not weave the web.

A witch once spoke of a prophecy that a kind and gentle soul will bring the most combative of beasts together in peace.

Believe this person is you.

Many people will ask
you for help. Cast a spell
when needed, but show
them how you did it.

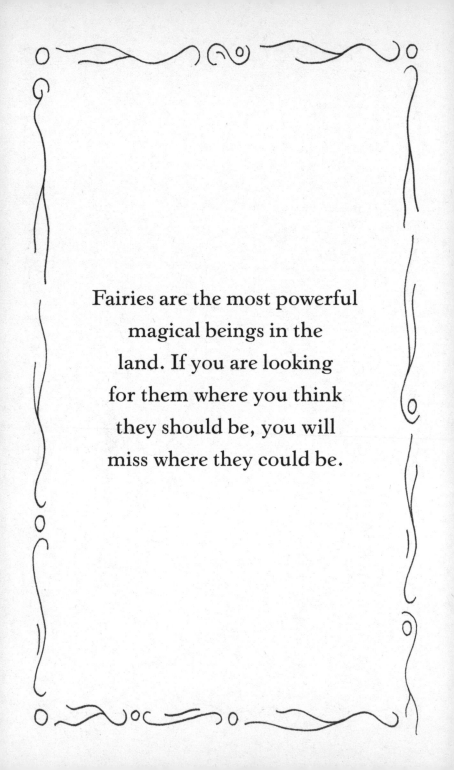

Fairies are the most powerful
magical beings in the
land. If you are looking
for them where you think
they should be, you will
miss where they could be.

The Pire and the Tall Man
can only stop wandering
when they are both satisfied.
The Pire always thinks he has
done his best magic and the
Tall Man always knows the
Pire can do better. Teach the
Pire to lose and the Tall Man
to win and they will tell you
the most magnificent stories.

There is a creature known
as the Bacradoll. It offers
a magical bottle to those
who are the angriest.

You can place your anger in
the bottle and the Bacradoll
offers to take it away. It may
seem as if the Bacradoll is
good. It is not. Once the
bottle is full, the Bacradoll
uses it to hurt those you love.

A levitation spell is helpful,
but you should understand
the weight of the burden
you are relieving.

If you truly love an Eyvel,
it will bring you great
joy. You must first see it
in its worst form. Only
then can you know if your
love is true indeed.

When you are feeling
lost, visit the Gargantuan
Lens of Midland Hills.

It will help you focus on the
task at hand and show you
what is truly important.

Music is one of the most
powerful forms of magic.

Learn it.

Swimming in the Sorrow
Pond will cause you to age,
get sick, and others to despise
you. Work as slowly as needed
toward shore. Ask for help
if you're stuck and a stick
will always be available.

A Gol Crystal is a children's toy with the power to teach and entertain. Use them sparingly as one was once used to trap the minds of the young.

The Unmovable Ram
cannot be pushed back
once it is charging towards
you. The more you try,
the stronger it gets. But if
you allow it to keep going,
it is easily swayed in any
direction you wish to go.

Magic exists whether
you believe it or not.

Believe it.

If a Flying Fleutle offers to carry you into the clouds, do not delay. The view from above will bring you great wisdom.

In the eastern corridor
basement there is a picture
of you with many others
hanging on the wall. It
is a test. Look at it. If
you see yourself last, you
will succeed and I will
have taught you well.

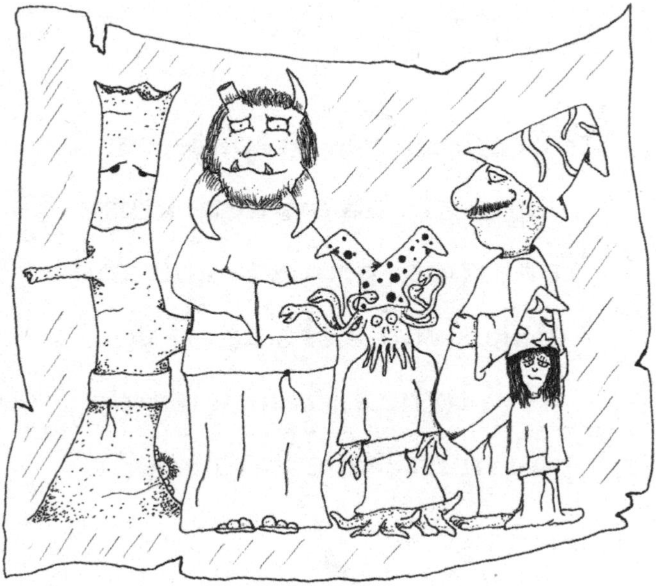

Your room was prepared with
magic when you were born.
Your room protects you and
makes you feel safe. If you
wish to be a great wizard,
you must leave your room.

You will be told many
fantastic tales. Listen to every
one. Ask questions until you
understand them. Do not
forget to write your own.

Copyright © 2015, 2022 by the phazelFOZ Company LLC
Cover and internal design © 2022 by Sourcebooks

Sourcebooks and the colophon are registered trademarks of Sourcebooks.

All rights reserved.

The characters and events portrayed in this book are fictitious or are used fictitiously. Any similarity to real persons, living or dead, is purely coincidental and not intended by the author.

Published by Sourcebooks eXplore, an imprint of
Sourcebooks Kids
P.O. Box 4410, Naperville, Illinois 60567–4410
(630) 961-3900
sourcebookskids.com

Originally published as *Mystical Rules for My Magical Daughter* in 2015 by the phazelFOZ Company LLC.

Library of Congress Cataloging-in-Publication Data

Names: Corchin, D. J., author, illustrator.
Title: If you find a unicorn, it is not yours to keep / DJ Corchin.
Other titles: Mystical rules for my magical daughter
Description: Naperville : Sourcebooks Explore, 2022. | "Originally published as Mystical Rules for My Magical Daughter in 2015 by the phazelFOZ Company LLC." | Summary: Illustrations and text offer a series of metaphorical life lessons for the magically inclined.
Identifiers: LCCN 2021054850 | (hardcover)
Subjects: CYAC: Magic--Fiction. | Conduct of life--Fiction. | Fantasy. | LCGFT: Picture books.
Classification: LCC PZ7.C812 If 2022 | DDC [E]--dc23
LC record available at https://lccn.loc.gov/2021054850

Source of Production: Versa Press, East Peoria, Illinois, USA
Date of Production: March 2022
Run Number: 5024776

Printed and bound in United States of America.
VP 10 9 8 7 6 5 4 3 2 1